Contents

I am a postman   4

Starting work   6

Sorting the mail   8

Getting ready to go   10

First deliveries   12

Safety   14

Birthday parcel   16

Special deliveries   18

Back to the delivery office   20

Helping people   22

When you grow up... & Answers   23

Glossary & Index   24

Words in **bold** are in the glossary on page 24.

KV-198-542

I am a postman

Hello, my name is Shaun and I am a postman.

Hello!

? What is your postman or postwoman's name?

I work for the **Royal Mail.**
We deliver lots of letters
and **parcels** to
people every day.

The letters and
parcels we deliver
are called '**post**'
or '**mail**'.

Starting work

I start work very early in the morning at 6:00am. The big Royal Mail lorries are already at the **delivery office**. They bring post to the delivery office every day so we can deliver it to **local** people.

I swipe my **security** badge on the card reader so I can get into the delivery office.

Why does the postman have a security badge?

Some of the other postal workers are already here.

Sorting the mail

I use a trolley to bring in some of the mail from one of the delivery lorries.

There is lots of post today.

Now I can put the post into area order. This will make it easier for me to sort it out into street order.

I take some post over to the sorting slots. There are slots for every street in my town.

These letters are going to Mountview Road, so I place them here. We have to look at the addresses carefully so we put them in the right slot.

Letters can have a **first-class stamp** or a **second-class stamp** on them.

MOUNTVIEW ROAD

Which will arrive sooner, a letter with a first- or a second-class stamp?

Getting ready to go

I've finished sorting the mail so I put it all into mailbags.

I collect my van keys and sign for my **special delivery** parcels. We sign for them so we know who is delivering them. Sometimes they contain **valuable** items.

I collect a **scanner** before I leave. People will sign their names on it when I deliver their special delivery parcels.

Phil also works as a postman here. We go out in the same van because our **rounds** are in the same area. We load the van together. We have to make sure that we wear our **reflective** jackets.

Why do you think postal workers wear reflective jackets on their rounds?

First deliveries

We arrive at the first street and get our mailbags out of the van.

The letters in my mailbag are all in order because I sorted them earlier.

I go to the first house I'm delivering to. I check each address carefully to make sure I post the right letters through the right door.

I push the letters through the letterbox.

Then I go to the next house. There are lots of letters for this one.

In you go!

?

Where is your letterbox?
Why is it important to make sure the letters are pushed through the letterbox carefully?

Safety

It's important for me to stay safe while I'm out delivering. Pet dogs live in lots of houses. Most dogs are friendly, but some of them aren't.

BEWARE OF DOG

I use a **posting stick** to put the mail through the door. This stops me from getting any nasty dog bites.

I also have to make sure that I'm protected from the Sun. I wear sun cream and a hat if it's hot. I keep water with me to make sure that I stay **hydrated** in hot weather.

Birthday parcel

There are balloons tied up outside the next house. It is somebody's birthday.

?

Have you ever received a birthday parcel in the post? What was in it?

Happy birthday!

I have birthday cards and a parcel for Storm. She is nine today. She is very excited about what might be in her parcel.

I deliver lots of birthday cards and parcels to people.

People who reach their 100th birthday get a card from Buckingham Palace. Inside is a birthday message from the Queen.

Special deliveries

I have two special deliveries. These are important and people must sign for them.

I knock on the door and ask the lady who lives there to sign on the scanner. This sends information back to the office to let them know the parcel has been delivered.

I knock on another door but there is nobody in. This special delivery will need to go back to the office.

I fill out a card to tell the person who lives here that I tried to deliver it.

I deliver a postcard to the next house.

Dear James,

We're having a lovely holiday in Greece. The weather is very hot and sunny. See you soon!

Lots of love,

Grandma & Grandpa

x x x

?

Who has sent the postcard? Where have they gone on holiday?

Back to the delivery office

Now we've finished our rounds, it's time to go back to the delivery office.

How did your round go today, Phil?

I hand the special delivery package back in so it can be put in a safe place.

I put my mailbags away ready for the next day.

? Why was the special delivery item brought back to the delivery office?

I check my hours on the **duties board** to see what **shifts** I'm working for the rest of the week.

It is 2:00pm and time for me to go home now.

Helping people

I really enjoy my job as a postman. I enjoy being active and working outside. Most of all, I enjoy making sure that people get their post delivered on time.

I really enjoy helping people!

When you grow up...

If you would like to be a postman or postwoman, here are some simple tips and advice:

What kind of person are you?

- You are friendly and helpful
- You are active and enjoy walking
- You are polite and well mannered
- You pay attention and can remember lots of details
- You enjoy being outside.

How do you become a postman or postwoman?

You don't need any special qualifications to become a postman or postwoman. You have to register online and take a test. You may then be asked for an interview and have to pass a security test before you can start delivering letters.

Answers

P7. The postman has a security badge because there are valuable items inside the delivery office.

P9. A letter with a first-class stamp will arrive sooner than one with a second-class stamp.

P11. Postal workers wear reflective jackets so they can easily be seen and because it is often dark when they start work.

P13. It is important to push the letters through the letterbox carefully because their contents can get damaged.

P19. Grandma and Grandpa sent the postcard. They went to Greece for their holiday.

P21. Special delivery items cannot be left on the doorstep because they may contain valuable items. They are brought back to the delivery office for safekeeping.

Were your answers the same as the ones in this book? Don't worry if they were different, sometimes there is more than one right answer. Talk about your answer with other people. Can you explain why you think your answer is right?

Glossary

delivery office the place where the post is brought to be sorted, ready for delivery

duties board a board that has all the times and days when postal workers have to work

first-class stamp this stamp is used for post that needs to be delivered quickly

hydrated to keep a healthy balance in your body by drinking enough water, especially when it's hot outside

local describes the area close to where you live

mail another word for post

parcel a larger item of post, usually too big to go through a letterbox

post the letters and parcels that postal workers deliver

posting stick a safety stick used to post letters to houses that may have dangerous dogs

reflective describes the material on clothing that reflects light so people can be seen at all times.

round the delivery route that a postman or postwoman does every day

Royal Mail a company that delivers the post all across the UK

scanner an electronic device that is used to collect signatures from people who have special deliveries

second-class stamp this stamp is used for post that does not have to be delivered quickly

security describes something that is used to keep a person or a place safe

shift the period of time when a postal worker has to work

special delivery important post that has to be signed for

valuable describes the post that might be very important or be worth a lot of money

Index

birthdays 16-17

deliveries 12-19

delivery office 6, 7, 18, 19, 20-21

dogs 14-15

letterboxes 13, 15

postcards 19

posting stick 15

reflective jackets 11

rounds 11, 20

Royal Mail 5, 6

Queen, the 17

safety 14-15

scanners 11, 18

security badge 7

shifts 21

sorting mail 8-9

special delivery items 10-11, 18-19, 21

stamps 9

sunscreen 15

water 15

Underwater Treasure

Written by Juliet Kerrigan

Contents

Exploring the underwater world	2
Underwater equipment	4
What happens in the water?	6
Ancient cargo	8
Tudor treasure	10
White gold	12
Doggerland	14
Seahenge	16
A lost city	18
Sword puzzle	20
Giants from the sea	22
Foreign gold	24
Old and new	26
Glossary	28
Index	29
Lost and found	30

Aberdeenshire

3186735

Exploring the underwater world

Archaeologists are interested in how people lived in the past. They've **excavated** on dry land for over 150 years, but there are a lot of valuable treasures to find underwater too.

Big objects in the water are sometimes spotted from planes, and experts go and have a look to see what's there. Sometimes archaeologists search underwater for something that's been described in books written hundreds or thousands of years ago.